The Golden Easter Egg

By Katherine Zwers and John Tobin

Illustrated by Carol Heyer

IDEALS CHILDREN'S BOOKS

Nashville, Tennessee

One early spring morning, many years ago, gentle rays of sunshine passed through the window of a small cottage in the woods. They played across the sleeping face of a little lamb named Hopscotch, gently awakening him from his peaceful slumber. This was the home of Sebastian the shepherd and his faithful companion Hopscotch.

"Today's the day!" Hopscotch shouted as he bounced off the sleeping Sebastian's tummy. Hopscotch was down the stairs and out the door before Sebastian could rub the sleep from his eyes.

"Ohhh no!" Sebastian exclaimed. "Here we go again!" And he grabbed his trusty staff and ran out the door after Hopscotch.

Sebastian ran across the meadow which was still wet with morning dew. There he found the little lamb bouncing from tree to tree in search of something.

"Hopscotch," Sebastian called, "what is all the commotion about this morning?"

"It's Easter!" Hopscotch excitedly replied. "It's Easter! And I'm looking for my Easter eggs."

Sebastian chuckled. "Hopscotch," he said, "today is Saturday. Easter is on Sunday. That's tomorrow!"

Hopscotch paused for a moment; Sebastian was right. Easter was still one more day away. Disappointed, Hopscotch ambled back to Sebastian's side.

An old mule who had been watching from the next pasture called out to Hopscotch. "Little lamb," he said, "I know where you can find the greatest Easter egg in the whole world . . . the Golden Easter Egg!"

The mule pulled a tattered old map from beneath his blanket. "This treasure map," he said, "was given to me by my last master, an old gold miner, as a reward for my many years of service. I want you to have it now."

"But why?" asked Sebastian.

"Because you have shown me much kindness in the past," replied the mule. "You gave me oats when I was hungry, and you covered me with blankets on cold winter nights."

Sebastian and Hopscotch thanked the mule and took the map home to begin planning their adventure.

"Hopscotch," said Sebastian, "the Golden Easter Egg seems to be on an island. I think we'll need a boat!"

That afternoon Sebastian and Hopscotch began building their adventure boat. They sawed and hammered and nailed all through the afternoon. Not until very late that night did they finish. Then Sebastian pulled out the old tattered map and laid it on the table. By the light of the candle, he carefully studied every detail of the map, planning their trip step by step.

The next morning, at first glimmer of light, Hopscotch was up and ready to go. As soon as Sebastian was on the boat, Hopscotch pulled and tugged until the heavy anchor released itself from the muddy bottom of the river.

"We're off!" Hopscotch shouted excitedly.

"So we are," Sebastian replied softly, for he was concerned about the outcome of their unlikely adventure. "So we are." He quietly pulled out the map and began to study it once more.

The boat began floating down the river. After a little while, they were floating through a jungle. Above their heads hung thick branches. The trees on the riverbank were full of colorful birds, and the ground was overrun with mysterious-looking plants.

"This is not as bad as I feared," Sebastian said to himself. "Perhaps the trip will turn out all right, after all."

But soon the jungle got thicker and seemed to close in around them. The sun disappeared from the sky, and it became very dark.

Hopscotch yelled, "Sebastian, look out! We're heading right for that cave!"

Sebastian tried desperately to stop the boat, but it was too late. The giant cave had already swallowed them up.

"Sebastian, where are we?" Hopscotch asked, his voice trembling.

"I'm not sure," Sebastian replied, trying to sound brave.

"Sebastian," Hopscotch said, "it's so dark in here . . ."

". . . so dark in here . . . so dark in here . . .," the cave echoed back.

The boat drifted further and further into the cave. All around them eyes glowed in the darkness, and strange noises echoed through the cave.

"Oh no! We're lost," Hopscotch said, and he began to cry.

Sebastian looked around and swallowed hard. The glowing eyes seemed to be getting closer.

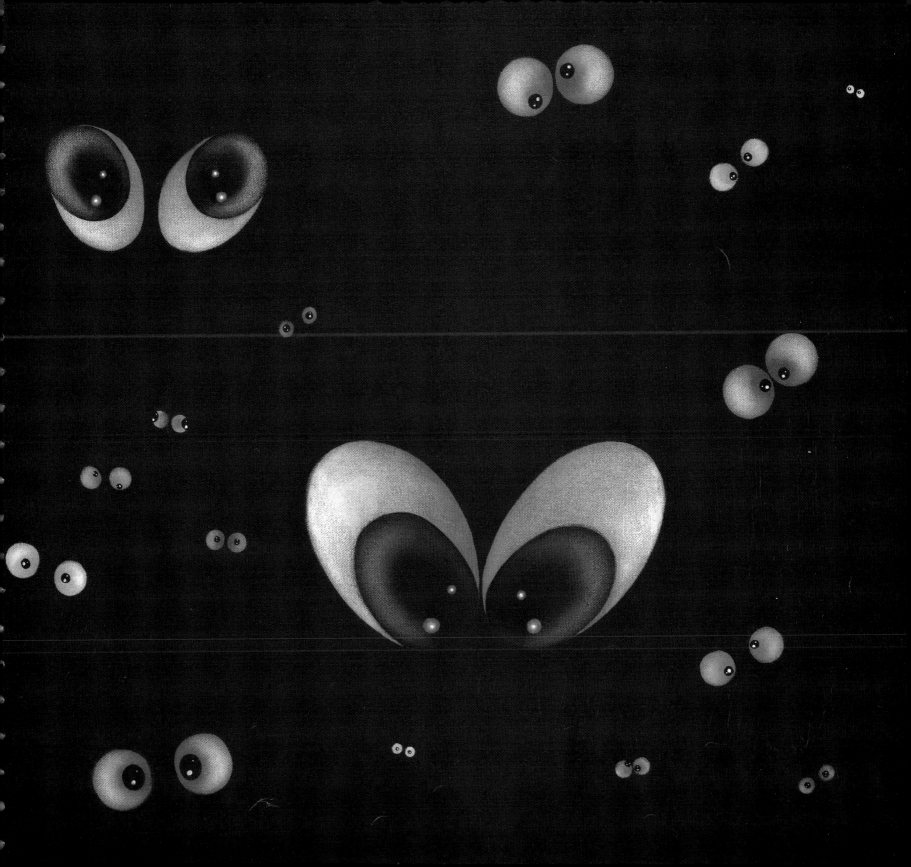

"Maybe I can help," came a tiny voice from the darkness. "My name is Sparkle." Slowly out of the darkness drifted a small yellow glow which became brighter and brighter until it lit up the entire front of the boat.

"Hi!" said Sebastian. "Are we ever glad to see you! As you can see, we are completely lost. We have this map, but we seem to have made a wrong turn somewhere."

The little firefly flew over to the map and studied it carefully. "Don't worry," he said. "I know just how to help you. I'll be your light and lead you out of the cave."

"Oh, how wonderful!" exclaimed Hopscotch. "Now we will be able to safely return to the river and continue our journey."

"Thank you, Sparkle," Sebastian shouted to the front of the boat as he steered his way out of the brightly lit cave. Sebastian and Hopscotch smiled at each other — they were safe again.

Suddenly the river began to move quickly. What had once been a calm and steady river now turned into a violent, rolling mass of water. Sebastian climbed up to the small crow's nest at the top of the mast. Just ahead he saw a giant twisting whirlpool. Before they could turn the boat around, Sebastian and Hopscotch were caught in its strong pull and were being sucked downward.

"Help! Help!" shouted Hopscotch.

"Hold on!" screamed Sebastian as he clung tightly to his little friend.

Luckily, a giant water turtle who was sunbathing nearby heard their cries for help. He quickly swam beneath the boat, and with one mighty push, he lifted the sinking boat from the swirling water and guided it safely to shore.

"Thank you, kind turtle," Sebastian said gratefully.

"You're welcome, my friends," the turtle replied. "But whatever are you doing floating down this river?"

"We are trying to follow this treasure map," said Sebastian as he pulled the water-soaked map from his pocket. "Perhaps you can show us where we are."

"Let me see," said the turtle as he looked at the map. "Hmmm. . . You must follow the stream straight ahead until you reach the Golden Forest."

So Sebastian and Hopscotch set off again.

It was late afternoon when the tiny boat reached the shore of the Golden Forest. Sebastian and Hopscotch stared up at the trees in wonderment. Never before had they seen such a beautiful place.

Sebastian pulled out the map and began searching for more clues to the Golden Easter Egg's hiding place.

But Hopscotch, already three steps ahead of Sebastian, began yelling, "I've found it! I've found it!"

And there, hidden in an old oak tree, sat the perfectly shaped Golden Easter Egg, a keyhole in its side. Beside it hung a key.

Sebastian carefully unlocked and opened the Golden Easter Egg, his eyes widening as he looked inside. The egg was filled to the top with every treat imaginable. Toys and candy of every description were waiting for Sebastian and Hopscotch. But also inside the egg was a small birdcage in which sat a small white dove.

Soon Hopscotch had eaten all the candy. "Ohhh," he groaned as he held his aching stomach, "is that all there is to Easter?"

"No, that's not all Easter is," Sebastian said with a gentle smile. He walked over to the cage.

"This is Easter!" Sebastian exclaimed as he opened the cage and set the tiny bird free.

High into the afternoon sky it flew, free at last.

"Easter," said Sebastian, "is the freedom of God's love."

Tired now, the gentle shepherd and his lamb walked back to their little boat, cradling in their arms the Golden Easter Egg and the empty little birdcage.

The End

Published by Ideals Publishing Corporation
Nelson Place at Elm Hill Pike
Nashville, Tennessee 37214

ISBN 0-8249-8322-X